We acknowledge the support of the Canada Council for the Arts, the Ontario Arts
Council, and the participation of the Government of Canada/la participation du
gouvernement du Canada for our publishing activities.

Original title: *La plus grosse poutine du monde*
Originally published by: ©2013 Bayard Canada Livres Inc.

Cataloging in Publication

Poulin, Andrée
[Plus grosse poutine du monde. English]
     The biggest poutine in the world / Andrée Poulin.
Translation of: La plus grosse poutine du monde.
Translated by Brigitte Waisberg.
Issued in print and electronic formats.
ISBN 978-1-55451-826-5 (bound).--ISBN 978-1-55451-825-8 (paperback).--
ISBN 978-1-55451-827-2 (epub).--ISBN 978-1-55451-828-9 (pdf)
     I. Waisberg, Brigitte, translator II. Title. III. Title: Plus grosse
poutine du monde. English.
PS8581.O837P6813 2016   jC843'.54   C2015-905357-9
                                                  C2015-905358-7

Published in the U.S.A. by Annick Press (U.S.) Ltd.
Distributed in Canada by University of Toronto Press.
Distributed in the U.S.A. by Publishers Group West.

Printed in Canada

Visit us at: www.annickpress.com

Also available in e-book format.
Please visit www.annickpress.com/ebooks.html for
more details. Or scan

The Biggest Poutine in the World

Andrée Poulin

Translated by Brigitte Waisberg

To Geneviève Gareau
who has instilled the love
of reading in so many
children.

Thank you to
Mme Viviane Desparois's
Grade 5 class for their
very helpful comments on
my manuscript.

The Biggest **Poutine** in the World

Andrée Poulin

Translated by Brigitte Waisberg

annick press
toronto • berkeley • vancouver

Conquering My Fear of Heights

Don't look down. Don't think about your sweaty hands slipping on the rungs of the ladder.

Just move one foot at a time. Try not to shake. Don't listen to your heart beating like a crazed tennis ball. And whatever you do, don't look down.

When you're standing with both feet on the ground, the water tower looks high. When you have both feet on the rungs of a ladder going up, you know that the water tower is *really* high. At forty meters up in the air, I feel small, scared, pathetic.

If I fall from this height, will I bash my brains in? I wonder what bashed-in brains lying on concrete look like. Sam shouts up from below, "Hey, Thomas! Come on! You're as slow as a turtle."

Today is my twelfth birthday. Because we wanted to have a bit of excitement on my birthday, and because the summer is already dragging in our sleepy Quebec town, Sam and I decided to climb the water tower. We're going to take our pictures up there and post them on Facebook. That'll impress our soccer team.

After ten minutes of climbing, I finally reach the top. My muscles are starting to relax just a little. My chest still feels tight, but I'm also bursting with pride. I've conquered my fear of heights! I made it!

I take a quick glance down. Sam, who looks no bigger than an elf, is taking pictures. I give him a small wave. I feel like I'm on top of the world.

Five Pine-Green Candles

At the bottom of my cupboard, I've hidden an old shoe box under a pile of clothes I've outgrown. There are five pine-green candles in it. Over time, they've lost a bit of their sheen. Two of the five candles have traces of dried brown gravy on them.

Every so often, I open the box and tell myself, "Her fingers touched these candles."

I know it's stupid, but it makes me feel closer to her.

If our house caught on fire, those five pine-green candles are the first things I'd save.

Once in a Lifetime

I know that my mother's not dead. Every year on my birthday, she sends me a letter. Well, not exactly a letter. An envelope. With a few dirty, crumpled $10 bills in it. And always the same words scribbled on a piece of paper:

Happy Birthday,
Thomas

Your mother

Every year for the past seven years, I've dreamed of getting a real letter. With news about my mother. Where she's living. What she's doing. I would even be happy with a simple sentence like, *I hope you're okay. I think of you often.*

Every year, I hold out hope, and every year, I'm disappointed. Maybe today? Who knows. Things can change. It's my lucky year. It only happens once in a lifetime—the year when your age is the same as the date you were born. Today, July 12, I'm turning twelve. Maybe my mother will realize that. She might even call me.

A glimmer of hope lights up in my mind. A tiny, fragile, trembling glimmer. I try not to pay too much attention to it. I've tasted disappointment before, and it doesn't taste good.

Paralyzed by Fear

It takes me as long to climb down the water tower as it did to climb up. When my feet finally touch the ground, I'm as dizzy as if I'd just had a turn on the Catapulte ride at La Ronde amusement park in Montreal. Sam approaches, raises his hand, and gives me a high five.

"My ninety-five-year-old great-grandmother could have made it up faster than you!" he says.

"We'll see if you can do any better," I reply.

Sam hands me the camera and jumps onto the ladder. He starts off climbing slowly but steadily. When he reaches the middle, he stops. I shout, "Who's the turtle now?"

No answer. I wait. Sam sticks his arms between the rungs of the ladder. "Bernier, what are you doing?" I call out.

Still no answer. Sam bends over and throws up the three pieces of toast he had for breakfast. Yuck! I shout up again, "Come down, Sam. Come on."

He still doesn't move. I wait for a couple of minutes. I don't have a choice. I'm going to have to go back up. Once I reach him halfway up the ladder, I calmly say, "Sam, I'm behind you. Come down."

My friend is shaking so hard I'm afraid he'll fall.

I put my hand on his foot. He yelps like a terrified puppy. "Don't touch me!"

How long does this last? I don't know. I tell him a hundred times to come down. He doesn't want me to touch him. He doesn't want to—or can't—move. He's completely paralyzed by fear. I'll never convince him.

I climb back down, take out my cell phone, and call Sam's mother. Luckily, it's early and she hasn't left for work yet. Despite my panicked babbling, Léa Bernier stays calm.

"I'm coming," she says.

The Emptiness That Hurts

Sam is terrified of the void below. I can understand.
I hate the emptiness too. A lot of people think that
empty space is just a hole or something missing.
Wrong. For me, it's like a burn. It hurts so much that it
twists my guts inside out. I've been carrying this pain
around for years. Most of the time, I manage to control
it, but on some days, it comes back to haunt me.

The Bear Hug

With a screech of tires that makes the gravel fly up, Sam's mother arrives in the lane that leads to the water tower. She jumps out of her car and runs toward the ladder. When she reaches Sam, she puts her hand on his ankle. Stuck halfway up the ladder between the earth and the sky, they stand there for several minutes. Several LONG minutes. I can't hear what Léa is saying to Sam, but she must have found the right words to reassure him because he's finally coming down, at a snail's pace. When he lands on the ground, he's shaking all over. His mother gives him a hug, a real bear hug. If my friend didn't die of fright on the ladder, he now risks dying of suffocation. Tears streaming down her face, Léa keeps repeating the same words, "My baby! My baby!"

I'm caught between relief and fury. Relieved to see Sam safe and sound on the ground. Furious that I have no one to give me a bear hug. The painful emptiness comes back to twist my insides.

Do Trees Like Chocolate Cake?

After all the excitement and emotions at the water tower, my house seems sadly quiet. Usually, the mess and dust don't bother me, but today I find them depressing.

I spend the rest of the morning waiting around by the phone. It doesn't ring. The mailman sticks two bills in the mailbox. Nothing for me. I'm not surprised. The envelope that my mother sends for my birthday usually shows up in the mailbox, but it's never delivered by the mailman. There's never a stamp or postmark on it.

In the afternoon, my father comes home with a store-bought triple chocolate cake. Most days, as soon as he comes home from work, he rushes to his workshop to work on his sailboat. He devotes all his free time to this old boat that he's been refurbishing for years. Today, however, he suggests a game of table hockey. It bugs me when he pretends to act like a father.

Especially because he's a bad actor. But I don't feel like arguing today, so I agree to play.

We play in earnest, without speaking or laughing. My father rarely laughs. After three boring games, I call it quits. My father doesn't argue. Still no phone call. I try not to think of Sam's mother's voice when she kept repeating, "My baby. My baby." There was so much feeling in her voice that it hurts me to remember it. I send my friend a text to see if he's feeling better.

Thomas: You okay? Feeling better?

Sam: Feel like a jerk. Don't know why I panicked.

Thomas: Next time, don't eat before.

Sam: Ha-ha.

Thomas: Send me pics.

Sam: Okay.

Thomas: Go roller-blading later?

Sam: Can't. Being punished.

Thomas: 😆

Sam: Does your dad know what happened?

Thomas: Doesn't know a thing.

Sam: Lucky!

Not that lucky. Who wants a father who's as present as a gust of wind? As talkative as a fire hydrant? As funny as a grammar class?

If my father found out that I had climbed to the top of the water tower, he wouldn't even bother yelling at me. If you're going to lecture somebody, you have to at least be interested in him.

Frozen pizza for dinner. My father glances at his sailing magazine lying on the corner of the table. He's trying not to give in to the temptation to read while eating. That's only because it's my birthday. The pizza tastes like pepperoni cardboard. My father puts the triple chocolate cake on the table. We don't have any candles. It doesn't make any difference because my father never sings. I eat two huge slabs of cake, which make me feel sick. Even though I've eaten too much, I still feel like there's a hole in my stomach.

My father gives me a check for my birthday, like he always does. With a check, he doesn't have to rack his brains to find something that I'll like. In a halting voice, he asks, "Do you want to go see a movie in Granby?" Granby, which is a little bigger than Sainte-Alphonsine, is where the nearest theater is.

He feels like going to a movie about as much as having a skunk in his bed. The last time we went to a movie together, he fell asleep.

"I was going to go roller-blading with the guys," I say.

Relieved, my father retreats to his workshop. I spend all evening walking in circles. The phone remains silent. I feel like throwing it against the wall. At midnight, my father comes out of his workshop. He's bent over and shuffling his feet. He looks like a bear coming out of its den. He goes up to bed without wishing me good night. I check the mailbox one last time. Empty.

Okay, I admit it. That thing about a lucky year is dumb. Turning twelve on July 12 has nothing to do with luck. It means absolutely nothing—zero.

I feel like breaking dishes. I walk out to the garden and throw the rest of the cake against a tree. That doesn't calm me down. I don't know how to get rid of that burning emptiness.

By two in the morning, I accept the unacceptable. My mother isn't going to call me this year either. She even forgot to send me her usual letter with its pathetic message.

So long, glimmer of hope. I look up at the millions of stars twinkling in the sky. I'd like to join them. Out in space, you can scream as much as you want. There's no one to hear you.

Poutine with Candles

On my fifth birthday, instead of a cake, my mother made me poutine. First, she peeled the potatoes. An entire bagful. She cried the whole time she was peeling them.

"Mom, it's onions that are supposed to make you cry," I said. She smiled at me through her tears.

We went together to buy curds, those yummy little lumps of cheese. My mother held my hand till we got to Ladouceur's Cheese Shop. Her hand was cool despite the July heat. At the store, my mother explained, "If the curds go *squeak*, *squeak* when you eat them, that means they're fresh."

Back home, I helped make the gravy. She fried the potatoes in a huge pot. I can still hear the cheerful sizzle of the fries in the oil. Then she scooped the cheese curds and the fragrant gravy on top of the fries.

Once the poutine was ready, my mother stuck five candles into the mountain of fries. Five pine-green candles. She sang "Happy Birthday" while tears rolled down her cheeks. My father was at work, but I couldn't have cared less that he wasn't there.

That night, my mother tucked me in, then sat down on the floor beside my bed. Her hair smelled like the oil from the fries. With my eyes half shut, I could see her silhouette on the wall. I thought it was weird that she stayed so long beside me in the dark. I couldn't understand why she was crying for the third time that day. The next morning, when I got up, she was gone. I haven't seen her since.

Can the Click of a Mouse Change Your Life?

The day after your birthday is never fun. Especially when your birthday was a complete bust. By the time I get up, my father is long gone to the bakery. The kitchen stinks of cold pizza. The dirty plates are still on the table. There's no milk for my cereal. No butter for my toast. I slam the cupboard doors shut.

I take out a bag of frozen French fries and empty it onto a cookie sheet. While the fries are warming up in the oven, I prepare a package of gravy. I don't have cheese curds so I cut up some mozzarella and put it on top of the reheated fries. I pour gravy over the whole thing.

I take out the shoe box and stick the five pine-green candles into my birthday poutine. But I don't light them.

Since no one sang "Happy Birthday" to me yesterday, I might as well do it myself. Actually, I don't sing, I scream. Because if I don't scream, I'll end up throwing the dirty dishes against the wall.

I eat my poutine while playing Angry Birds on the computer. I took the fries out of the oven too soon. They're still cold in the middle. The gravy is lumpy and the cheese hasn't melted all the way. To help this disgusting meal go down, I click on one of my favorite sites, Guinness World Records.

Under the category "Most Popular Records" is Alastair Galpin of New Zealand who holds the record for the most weight lifted by a human tongue: 1.7 kilos. He also holds the record for eating the biggest bowl of soup: 25,000 litres.

I try to imagine a giant bowl of soup. Then my gaze falls on my half-eaten poutine. An idea sprouts in my mind. What if I tried to break a world record? How about a giant poutine? A really good poutine like the one my mother made me. That's it! I need a project. No more walking around in circles in this dusty, silent house. I'll set a record. Show that I'm not a loser who was abandoned by his mother and lives with a cold, distant father.

Yes! Yes! Yes! I, Thomas Gagné will get into the *Guinness World Records* book. The more I think of it, the more I like the idea. I click on the registration form.

My teacher says that a single beat of a butterfly's wings can set off a tornado at the other end of the world. Is it the same for a click of a mouse? Can a single click change your life? Let's hope so. My life needs to change.

For the first time since I turned twelve, I no longer feel like breaking dishes. I hop up and down with excitement in front of my computer. I'm going to make the biggest poutine in the world!

The biggest poutine in the world

A 650-Kilo Poutine

In less than an hour, I've planned it all out. I've even found a good name for it: the Phenomenal Poutine Project, PPP for short. I've decided to aim for 650 kilos.

Here are the ingredients I'll need for my giant poutine:

300 kilos of French fries

150 kilos of cheese curds

200 kilos of gravy

With 650 kilos of poutine, I'll be able to feed hundreds of people. It'll be a huge French fry feast. I'll have to find a place to hold the event. And some sponsors.

All the media will be talking about the kid from Sainte-Alphonsine, Quebec, who made the biggest poutine in the world. I'll give TV and radio interviews. My picture will be in all the papers. My video will go viral on YouTube. I'll get thousands of new friends on Facebook. And the cherry on top: my picture in the *Guinness World Records* book.

Maybe when I become famous, my father will finally show some interest in me. Maybe my mother will hear about her celebrity son. Maybe she'll call to congratulate me. Maybe we'll see each other again. That's a lot of "maybes," but it doesn't cost anything to hope. And today, hope makes me feel like flying.

Hundreds of Questions, Zero Answers

A thick cloak of mystery surrounds my mother. Why did she leave? Where does she live? What did she do to my father that he hates her so much? What did I do to make her abandon me?

Hundreds of questions, zero answers. Same thing for those so-called letters for my birthday. Who brings them? For a long time, I thought my father was playing at being the mailman. But every year, when I find the envelope in the mailbox, he's as shocked and surprised as me. My father is a really bad liar, so I'd know right away if he was in on it.

Sometimes I wonder if that lousy envelope is really from my mother at all. Maybe it's someone from the village who thinks he's Santa Claus or the Tooth Fairy and wants to cheer up that poor little Gagné boy without a mother?

Just thinking about it makes the hair on the back of my neck stand on end. Pity makes me sick.

· ·

Sam: Going to soccer practice?

Thomas: Yeah. Send pics from water tower.

Sam: Anything else?

Thomas: A small favor. It involves your godfather.

Sam: ???

Thomas: Will explain later.

Sam: Now!!

Thomas: Patience.

Sam: 😡

The First Volunteers

Every Friday night, after practice, the soccer team meets at the corner store for ice cream. As usual, the guys are wound up and goofing around. I have to shout to make myself heard. But as soon as I say "Guinness world record," I have their attention. When I tell them about my Phenomenal Poutine Project, they all start talking at once.

650 kilos of poutine isn't all that big. I could eat at least 100 kilos by myself.

It's going to cost you a lot to make that.

How many people can you feed with that much?

33

The guys are on board. Phew! I've already got a dozen volunteers. To make the Phenomenal Poutine Project happen and to get the record validated, I'm going to need help. Lots of help. Before, during, and after. Sam is the only one who surprises me a little. He's the only one who doesn't react.

Crazy About the *Guinness World Records* Book

Once all the guys have left, Sam finally decides to speak.

"You could have told me before," he says.

"Sam, I only got the idea this morning!"

"You don't tell me anything about your big plans and then you ask me to help you."

Still angry, Sam kicks the tires of his bike, then continues: "I've already figured out what favor you want me to ask my godfather for."

"Good going, Sherlock. Do you think he'll sponsor me for the fries?"

"Maybe . . . If I help you, can I get my picture in the *Guinness World Records* book too?"

"Hmmm . . . We'll see."

We ride to Frank's French Fries truck, right in the middle of Main Street in Sainte-Alphonsine.

In front of his truck, Fat Frank (FF to his friends) is circling around his newly purchased used car, as excited as a kid on Christmas morning. His belly is quivering under his too-tight T-shirt. Sam's godfather is crazy about (let's just say obsessed by) old cars.

"It's a 1957 Ford Fairlane. This beauty cost me an arm and a leg, but she's in perfect condition!" declares Fat Frank.

I can't understand why anyone would spend so much money for an old lemon-yellow convertible. But Fat Frank makes a lot of money with his five poutine trucks. There are always lineups in front of Frank's, which is known as the best poutine chain in the area.

Sam spends a long time admiring the body of the Ford Fairlane, oohing and aahing in front of the hubcaps. I nudge him in the ribs to remind him why we're here.

"Hey, FF, have I ever told you that you're the best godfather in the world?"

Fat Frank bursts out laughing.

"Geez, Sam, you're never going to win any prizes for subtlety. What do you need?"

"Three hundred kilos of French fries."

"What! Are you planning on feeding a dozen giants?" asks FF.

"I'm serious. It's for the PPP," declares Sam.

"The what?"

"The Phenomenal Poutine Project."

As soon as I mention the word Guinness, Fat Frank interrupts my explanation.

"The *Guinness World Records* book!? My favorite book. When I was your age, I must have read it at least fifty times."

He agrees right away to supply me with three hundred kilos of fries. Had I known he'd say yes so easily, I would have asked him for an iPad too.

"Thanks, FF. There's no one like you!" says Sam as he gives him a punch on the shoulder. Fat Frank gives him one back. The two of them are happily pushing each other around in front of the truck. Sam is hopping back and forth like a boxer, laughing like a hyena. Dumb.

Once again, I'm torn between relief and jealousy. Relief at having gotten the sponsorship for the fries. Jealousy about not having a godfather who's as funny as a clown and as generous as Cinderella's fairy godmother. The emptiness that hurts makes my insides twist.

Five Pieces . . . Then Ten

The envelope arrived three days late. I found it this morning in the mailbox. It was even worse than before: there was only one dirty, crumpled $10 bill in it. My mother stuck a candy-pink Post-it note on it with the same stupid message: Happy Birthday, Thomas. Your mother.

I grab a dirty plate from the sink, go out, and smash it on the front walk. The plate breaks into five pieces. I pick them up and throw them into the garbage can. I like the clatter of broken dishes.

Then I tear the $10 bill into ten little pieces, which also make their way into the garbage. The ten pieces of the bill fall silently onto the five pieces of the plate. Breaking, tearing . . . little ways to vent, but they don't do much good. I jump onto my bike and race over to Ladouceur's Cheese Shop. I'm going to make the biggest poutine in the world, win a Guinness world record, and show my mother what a dumb-ass move she made when she threw me out of her life.

Irene Ladouceur Sets a Condition

Once I'm in front of the cheese shop, I realize that I haven't thought about what I'm going to say to convince the owner. If Mederic Ladouceur were still alive, I would have gotten him to sponsor me just by snapping my fingers. Old Mederic loved sailboats and spent hours in the workshop with my father. Anyway, the master cheese-maker died six months ago and his niece has taken over the business.

When she arrived this spring, Irene Ladouceur set the tongues of all Sainte-Alphonsine's gossips wagging. Did this niece from Montreal really know anything about cheese?

Irene Ladouceur's daughter is sitting in front of the cheese shop reading *Asterix at the Olympic Games*. Eliane Ladouceur was a big topic of conversation at our school. Because she's "different," everyone tried their best to avoid her.

Even though it's twenty-five degrees Celsius, Eliane is wearing a blouse with long sleeves that go right down over her hands. When I get near her chair, our eyes meet. She gives me a faint smile and says, "Hi." I pretend I didn't hear her.

When I ask to see the owner, the cashier sends me to the back where I find Irene Ladouceur, a tall woman, thin and pale like her cheese sticks. She's not old, but her white paper cap makes her look like a grandma. I get right to the point.

"I want to set a Guinness record for the biggest poutine in the world. I'm looking for sponsors. I'd be the happiest kid in the world if you would supply me with a hundred and fifty kilos of cheese curds."

She lets out a whistle.

"At $18 a kilo, that comes to $2,700. That's quite the sponsorship."

"Your uncle would have said yes."

She raises an eyebrow into a point.

"How do you know?"

"He and my father were good friends."

Irene Ladouceur fiddles with a bag of cheese. She's still unsure.

"My record is going to attract journalists," I continue. "The newspapers, radio, and TV will all be talking about your cheese shop. It'll be great publicity. And the people of Sainte-Alphonsine will be touched by your generosity."

She smiles and says, "You've made some pretty good arguments there."

Irene Ladouceur takes off her cap, wipes her sweaty brow, and says, "Okay. But on one condition."

"What's that?" I ask.

"That you include my daughter in your project," she replies.

Oh no! Not a girl in the project! And Eliane Ladouceur to boot! The guys on the soccer team are going to squawk.

"Umm . . . I don't think your daughter would be interested in my project," I say.

Irene Ladouceur insists:

"Starting school in Granby wasn't easy for Elie."

Who's stupid enough to move at the beginning of June, just before the end of the school year! All the kids have been in groups for a long time. If she wasn't so weird, maybe Eliane Ladouceur would have found it easier to make friends and be part of a group. But her hand . . .

"She doesn't know anyone here. I don't want her to spend the summer alone," adds Irene Ladouceur.

I don't have a choice. If I want her to pay for the cheese, I have to accept her condition.

In a solemn voice, as if I'm 100 percent sincere, I say, "Your daughter is welcome to join my project."

Irene Ladouceur gives me a big smile and a bag of cheese curds. I go out through the side door to avoid her daughter reading in front.

Thomas: You free after dinner?

Sam: Yeah.

Thomas: I'm coming over. Good news about PPP.

Sam: ???

Thomas: Bad news too.

Sam: ???

Thomas: Will explain later.

Sam: Now!!!

Thomas: Patience.

Sam: 🙁

. . . .

A Real Family Laughs Together

When I get to Sam's, the Berniers have finished eating, but Léa makes me sit down at the table and puts a plate of shepherd's pie in front of me. Léa has known me since I was a baby, so she knows that at my house meals center around frozen food.

"Eat up, Thomas! You're thinner than a broomstick," she says.

"Léa would like it if everyone had love handles as beautiful as hers," says Sam's father as he gives his wife a kiss on the neck. She responds with a playful punch on his shoulder.

"We have serious things to discuss. Things that the adults shouldn't hear," states Sam.

His father breaks out laughing and kisses Sam on his cheek.

"Yuck!" shouts Sam, pretending to be angry.

His parents go outside, each carrying a book. That's what a real family looks like. Laughing. Teasing. Those are ways of saying, I'm interested in you enough to try and make you laugh. Not like my place where there's just silence and nobody cares.

"Start with the good news," says Sam.

"I have a sponsor for the cheese!"

He high-fives me.

"Yesss! And the bad news?

"Irene Ladouceur agreed to sponsor me on one condition: that I include her daughter in our plans."

"Eliane Ladouceur? No one talks to her at school."

"I know . . ."

"And her hand . . ."

"I don't have a choice."

Frustrated, he shakes his head.

"Anyway, it's your problem. As for me, I'm keeping far away from her. So what now?"

I take a mouthful of shepherd's pie to give me time to think of the best way of presenting things.

"I want you to come and see the mayor with me," I say.

He raises his eyes to the sky.

"Oh no! Why?"

"I need the arena to prepare and serve my poutine."

"Can't we do it outside?"

"Outside? With all the rain we get around here? Can you see me preparing 650 kilos of poutine and serving it in the middle of a storm? In the arena, there's lots of room to put big tables, and we can use the hot plates in the cafeteria for the gravy."

Sam is grumbling under his breath. I expected as much. The mayor is his neighbor and he's had to put up with her strange behavior for a long time.

"Grrr . . . Tartatcheff. I can't stand her," he mutters.

"I know. But this Guinness record isn't going to land in

our laps. You're her neighbor. If you ask her, we'll have a better chance of her saying yes."

"If I go, will you promise me that I'll get my picture in the *Guinness World Records* book?"

"You're really obsessed with this picture thing! Come on. Let's go."

A Rude Parrot

When we get to Thérèse Tartatcheff's, we can hear cries through the slightly open door: "Imbecile! Clumsy reptile!"

I whisper to Sam, "Her parrot needs a lesson in manners."

My friend sighs in exasperation. "The best way to insult the mayor is by calling her bird a parrot. As she says about one hundred and seventy-five times a week, her George is not an ordinary parrot. He's a Senegal parrot."

Thérèse Tartatcheff opens the door for us, and as is the case whenever I see her, I think she looks like a clown. It always surprises me that the citizens of Sainte-Alphonsine, who are so conservative, have elected her for the last ten years. Built like a truck driver, with a mop of dyed-red hair, the mayor always wears yellow clothes.

"Hello there, my little neighbor."

"Hello, Mrs. Tartatcheff," says Sam with a forced smile.

Then she turns to me.

"Are you Pierre Gagné's son?"

"Yes."

"That's what I thought. What can I do for you two?"

"We have a favor to ask you," says Sam, again with a forced smile.

The mayor invites us into her kitchen, which smells like overripe bananas. The Senegal parrot is sitting on his perch in an open cage. With his lime-green feathers and mango-yellow belly, I have to admit he's kind of cool. Too bad he's so miserable. As soon as he sees us, the parrot starts to scream: "Idiot! Illiterate! Ignoramus—"

"That's enough, George," scolds Tartatcheff in a harsh tone.

"It's about the arena," says Sam. "Thomas has a really great project—"

I start to explain all about my PPP, but as soon as I say the word poutine, the mayor jumps up as if she just sat on a porcupine.

"Stop! I've worked too hard to ban junk food at the arena to let you sell tons of fries there."

I explain, "We're not going to sell poutine, we're going to give it away."

"Besides," she continues, "I can't let you use the arena free of charge while other organizations have to pay. Sainte-Alphonsine needs the rental income."

The parrot screams:

NONO! IDIOT! NONO!

I elbow Sam. He's being as chatty as a wall. I try another argument:

"If I manage to break a Guinness record, they're going to talk about Sainte-Alphonsine on TV and in the papers. It'll be great publicity for the town—"

"Guinness or not, I don't want poutine in my arena," repeats Tartatcheff.

"Can't we at least—"

She interrupts by raising her hand, which is as large as a ping-pong paddle.

"Sorry, guys, I have to get ready for the tai chi class that I'm giving tomorrow morning. Thanks for your visit."

The cheeky parrot starts to holler again:

"Crrrrretin! Crrrrackpot! Complete crrrretin!"

If I wrung the mayor's neck and her parrot's, which one would scream louder?

Too Much Paperwork

From: rmt@guinnessworldrecords.com
To: TomG@me.com
July 18, 11:33 a.m.
File No. 322557
Member No. 283845

Dear Sir,

Thank you for submitting your proposal to establish a record for the biggest poutine in the world. Please find attached instructions for this record category as well as a kit outlining the requirements for completing your project and setting a record.

Yours sincerely,

Julie Smith
Guinness World Records
184–192 Drummond Street
London, England
NW1 3HP

Yeah, let's talk about their kit. I realize that the Guinness World Records comes from England, but they could have at least made an effort to make the forms easier to understand. I am going to spend weeks trying to get through them all.

Suddenly, a brilliant idea flashes in my mind. Eliane Ladouceur! Since I'm obligated to include her in my PPP, I'm going to give her these forms to take care of. She can't be as useless as me when it comes to paperwork. You never know: maybe she likes filling out forms?

Another Bird Drives Me Crazy

In a flash, I stuff the forms into my backpack and jump on my bike to ride to the Ladouceurs' house, just beside the cheese shop. I find Eliane on a lounge chair on the front lawn, busy reading *Asterix and Cleopatra*. Nearby, a turquoise bird in a cage is smoothing its feathers.

Eliane Ladouceur doesn't look up as I approach her, but I know she saw me.

"Hi," I say.

Nothing.

"Hi," I repeat louder.

She still doesn't look up. Her braid follows the curve of her arm like a long ribbon of chocolate.

"Uh-uh," she mumbles.

Finally, her majesty deigns to turn toward me.

"Frustrating, isn't it, to be ignored when you say hi to someone."

Uh-oh! She sounds hostile and looks angry. This is one unhappy girl. I stare at her feet to avoid looking at her hand.

"Uh . . . you said hi to me? When was that?" I ask.

"Don't play dumb," she replies. "You're only making things worse for yourself," she shoots back impatiently. "Yesterday, at the cheese shop, you ignored me. You're only speaking to me now because you need something."

I scratch a patch of rust on the handlebar. I'm sweating. If I had wings, I would fly away. The turquoise bird in the cage is making a little bell attached to a heart-shaped mirror tinkle.

I use it to change the subject.

"Does your bird like looking at itself in the mirror?"

She corrects me in a frosty voice:

"It's a budgie."

"Okay then, a budgie. Hey, do you know about my world record project?"

"I know that my mother is making you include me in your project in exchange for sponsoring the cheese," she replies.

"Uh . . . yeah."

In a harsh tone, she asks, "Do you really want me to take part?"

It's useless to pretend. She'll see right through me. I'm as bad a liar as my father.

"I don't have a choice," I say.

Eliane gives me a strange smile. It looks as if she can't decide whether to find that funny or sad. "Finally, a little bit of honesty," she says.

"The members of my soccer team promised to help. We're already a bunch of guys, you know?"

She shakes her head.

"No, I don't know," she exclaims. "I don't know why my hand bothers you so much, you and your friends and everybody else at school—"

"Uh . . . but . . . I . . ."

Suddenly, she stands up and throws her braid over her shoulder. Then she shakes her hand in front of my face.

"It's an artificial hand. It's not contagious. It's not going to bite anyone."

Eliane Ladouceur goes back into the house, slamming the door behind her. The budgie starts to squawk as if someone's pulling out its feathers. Obviously, I have no luck with females who like birds.

What Color Are Her Eyes?

Sam sent the pictures he took of me at the top of the water tower. When I look at myself perched so high on the ladder, I hear Léa Bernier's voice again: "My baby! My baby!"

What would my mother say if she saw that picture? Would she cry out in a voice full of fear, My baby! My baby! You mustn't do stupid things like that!

If my mother could see that picture, she probably wouldn't recognize me. I no longer look like a cute little five-year-old. And if I bumped into my mother at the store, would I recognize her?

I have blue eyes and my father's are brown. I have brown hair and my father's is black. Does my mother have blue eyes? I don't know. I can't remember. Is her hair brown? I don't know. I can't remember. I can't decide what hurts more, not knowing or not remembering.

Celery Brain

Now that I have confirmation from Guinness that I can go ahead, I've emptied my bank account: $200. I add the $40 my father gave me for my birthday. I borrow $20 each from three guys on the soccer team.

When I ask Sam if he'll lend me $40, he replies, "If you let me have my picture in the *Guinness World Records* book."

He's really starting to bug me with his demands. He lent me the money anyway. I have a total of $340 in my pocket, enough to reserve the arena.

Sam flatly refuses to come with me again to the mayor's house.

"Thérèse Tartatcheff is more stubborn than three mules. Good luck with making her change her mind. Even if you offered her $100,000, she wouldn't rent the arena to you."

To load the dice in my favor, I go to City Hall rather than

to the mayor's house. I take a banana for her parrot. Her secretary makes me cool my heels for thirty minutes. That'll teach me not to make an appointment. I can hear the bird chattering behind the office door.

The secretary sighs. "Sometimes I dream that George chokes on a piece of dried mango . . ."

By the time Mrs. Tartatcheff finally sees me, I've played around so much with the parrot's banana that it's lost its shape. The mayor invites me into her office with as much enthusiasm as if she were inviting a herd of elephants into her house.

Today she's wearing a dress the same color as the belly of her bird, which is perched on her shoulder.

"Hello, Thomas Gagné."

"Hello, ma'am. I've brought George a snack."

I give him the soft banana and place the pile of bills on her desk.

"Here's a deposit for renting the arena for a day at the beginning of August," I say.

Let's hope she doesn't notice that my hands are shaking. That crazy parrot starts to scream,

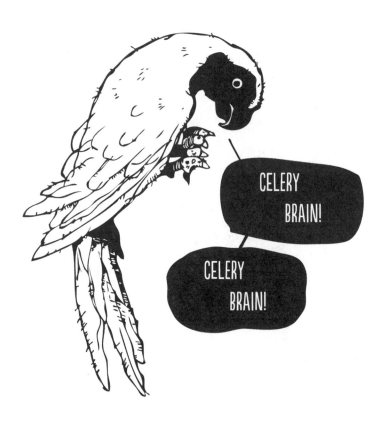

The mayor shakes her head and, carefully pronouncing every syllable, as if she were speaking to a child in kindergarten, she says, "I've already explained to you my position about junk food. No poutine in my arena. Even if you were to give me three times the regular rate, I wouldn't rent the arena to you."

"It's not your arena!" I shout.

Arching her eyebrows, she replies stiffly, "I am the mayor of Sainte-Alphonsine, and I'm the one who decides. Now, if you'll excuse me, I have important business to attend to."

Even after I've slammed the door behind me, I keep hearing the squawks of that big rude bird:

CELERY BRAIN!

CELERY BRAIN!

I ride around Sainte-Alphonsine on my bike to see if there are any other possible sites for my PPP. The school gym isn't big enough. The church basement is being renovated. Really, the arena is the best place— the only place—to do my project. How am I going to convince that stubborn Tartatcheff?

Avoiding Volcanoes

Seeing someone sob is ten times worse than watching them cry. When someone is crying, it's simple: tears run down. You can pretend that you didn't see them. But when someone is sobbing, it's like an erupting volcano. Impossible to stick your head in the sand.

When I was nine years old, my father let his volcano erupt. It was another July 12 when I had waited all day for my mother to show me some sign of life. I had found the usual envelope with the crumpled bills in the mailbox, but I wanted more. A real letter. With news. I wanted an e-mail, a call, a visit. I couldn't stand this fog of mystery any longer. So I had a temper tantrum. I kicked my feet. I screamed. My questions exploded like bombs in my father's face. "Why did she leave? Where is she living? Why doesn't she ever come to see us?"

In a trembling voice, my father responded, "She doesn't want to have anything to do with us."

His answer did nothing to calm me down. I continued to scream at the top of my lungs. My anger stirred the volcano that was sleeping inside my father. He began to make these weird groaning sounds, half muffled, as if he was about to throw up. When he began to sob, I immediately stopped yelling. With his bulging eyes, quivering lips, heaving shoulders, and snot running down his face, my father scared me. And the tears! Geez! Rivers of tears. He didn't even try to cover them up.

I was frozen with fear. There was no way I could console my father. Was he going to have a heart attack? Break into a thousand pieces? Flood the house with tears? The worst thing was that I had no idea how to stop the volcano. No idea how to comfort him.

Once you've seen someone cry so violently, you know that you should never stir the volcano again. That's why I don't know what made my mother leave us. Because of the volcanoes, I'm afraid to ask again. If I insist too much, my father could take his old sailboat and go to the other side of the planet, abandoning me as well.

A Lot of Hellos

Eliane Ladouceur is living in the time of the dinosaurs. She doesn't have a cell phone or a Facebook page. I had to phone her mother to get her e-mail address.

YOU HAVE MAIL

YOU HAVE MAIL

From: TomG@me.com
To: ElieLadouce@mymail.ca
July 19, 12:32 p.m.

Hi, Eliane Ladouceur,

Your mother gave me your e-mail address.

Okay. I admit it. I ignored you the other day.

It was dumb.

And stupid.

I'm sorry.

Here's the real truth: this Guinness World Record project is important to me. For reasons that I don't want to explain. That's why I need a sponsor for the cheese. Also, I need help with the Guinness forms. I can't pay you. All my savings are going into the PPP.

In exchange for your help, I'll give you my Asterix collection. Twelve books in excellent shape. It's a very generous offer.

Thomas

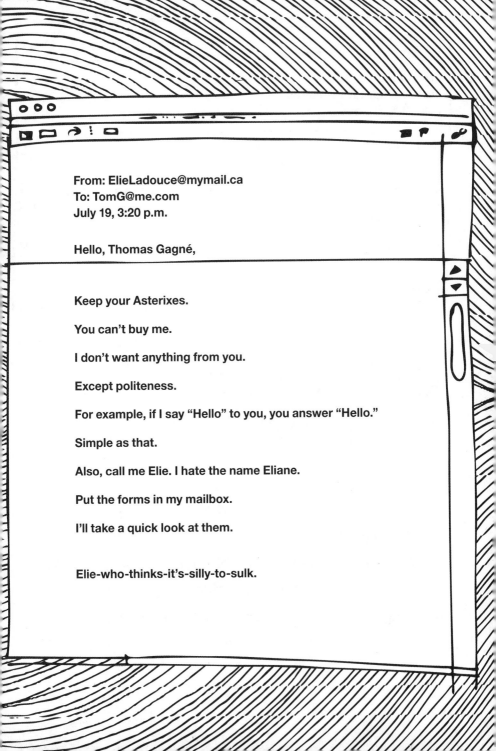

From: ElieLadouce@mymail.ca
To: TomG@me.com
July 19, 3:20 p.m.

Hello, Thomas Gagné,

Keep your Asterixes.

You can't buy me.

I don't want anything from you.

Except politeness.

For example, if I say "Hello" to you, you answer "Hello."

Simple as that.

Also, call me Elie. I hate the name Eliane.

Put the forms in my mailbox.

I'll take a quick look at them.

Elie-who-thinks-it's-silly-to-sulk.

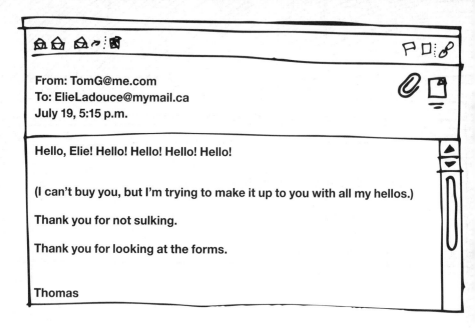

From: TomG@me.com
To: ElieLadouce@mymail.ca
July 19, 5:15 p.m.

Hello, Elie! Hello! Hello! Hello! Hello!

(I can't buy you, but I'm trying to make it up to you with all my hellos.)

Thank you for not sulking.

Thank you for looking at the forms.

Thomas

Did Asterix Eat Poutine?

For the Guinness World Records, I'm going to make a traditional poutine. With a simple brown gravy. But when I was looking for the recipe on the Internet, I found different versions of poutine. Just reading the list makes me hungry. One day, I'm going to try all of them.

Poutine Menu

Poutine Royale
(smoked sausage)

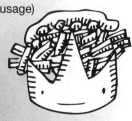

Cajun Poutine
(spicy fries)

Vegetarian Poutine
(mushrooms, peppers, and onions)

> Very healthy. Perfect for our mayor who hates junk food so much.

Crunchy Poutine
(bacon)

Poutine Bourguignon
(beef bourguignon, garlic, wine)

> Who would want to eat fries floating in wine?
>
> YUCK!

Teary-Eyed Poutine
(hot peppers and onions)

> I like the name . . .

French Poutine
(pepper sauce)

> I wonder if they eat this in Paris . . .

Italian Poutine
(spaghetti sauce)

Oktoberfest Poutine
(German sausage)

Obelix Poutine
(smoked meat)

Chicken Poutine
(chicken breast)

Roast Beef Poutine
(that's right, roast beef . . .)

Old-Time Poutine
(with peas, chicken, and cabbage)

Kamikaze Poutine
(hot sausage, hot peppers, and Tabasco sauce)

Pizza Poutine
(pepperoni, green peppers, mushrooms, and cheese)

73

Sam: Found a table for PPP. Yay!

Thomas: Who? What? How?

Sam: My neighbor. Best welder in town. Going to make a metal table.

Thomas: Size?

Sam: 4m x 1m. Perfect for 650 kilos of poutine.

Thomas: How much $$$?

Sam: Free. On loan.

Thomas: Awesome! Maybe you're not such a moron . . .

Sam: Want to be in photo for *Guinness World Records*!

Mystery of the Handcuffs

There are so many secrets about my mother that I can't even count them anymore. Of all the unanswered questions, the one that bugs me the most has to do with a pair of handcuffs.

When I was eight, Sam dressed up as a policeman for Halloween. His father bought him a pair of plastic handcuffs to go with his costume. When I saw the handcuffs hanging from my friend's belt, I broke out sobbing. I cried like a fountain without knowing why. Sam's mother hugged me tightly until I finally calmed down.

A few days later, I stole the handcuffs. They were just lying around in Sam's room. I still have them, hidden under my mattress. From time to time, I take them out, stare at them, and think really hard. But no matter how hard I try, I can't remember anything. The memories refuse to rise to the surface. The handcuffs are linked to my mother, I know that for sure. But I don't know why.

From: ElieLadouce@mymail.ca
To: TomG@me.com
July 21, 10:32 a.m.

Hi, Mr. Poutine,

Here is the list of instructions sent by Guinness:

- The poutine must be prepared in a sanitized container.
- Professional tools must be used to take all measurements.
- The weight of the plate must be subtracted from the final weight of the poutine. We recommend that the plate be weighed before the poutine is made.
- Please indicate the number of people who prepared the poutine as well as the number of hours required to prepare and cook it.
- All the ingredients used in the dish must be prepared under sanitary conditions so as to make them suitable for human consumption.
- All measurements must be supplied in metric and imperial units.

Elie-the-organizer

She hesitates for a moment, then says, "Do you want something to drink?"

I follow her into the kitchen. The turquoise budgie is perched on top of the fridge. As soon as it sees me, it starts to whistle aggressively.

Elie pours me a glass of juice.

"I really gave it to my mom for forcing you to include me in your project. She wants so much for me to be happy that sometimes she goes too far. Does your mother mix into your business like that?"

I bend down and do up my lace, which is not undone. I let it out really quickly:

"I haven't seen my mother in years."

Elie lifts her eyebrows.

"She never calls?"

"Never. No calls. No letters. No e-mails. Nothing but a little bit of cash for my birthday."

"How come?"

The Hand Swallowed by a Wolf

Rather than reply by e-mail, I quickly ride my bike to Elie's. When she opens the door, I hand her *Asterix in Belgium*. She takes the comic with her real hand, the left one. "Have you read it?" I ask her.

She shakes her head. "It's the best one," I add.

She smiles. For the first time, I notice the color of her eyes. Blue. Deep blue.

"Thank you," she says. "I'll let you know what I think."

I hop from one foot to the other.

"Your work on the Guinness forms is great. It'll help me get organized."

"I'll do the rest of it today."

"Thanks."

I try to ignore the pain in my stomach, the return of the emptiness that hurts. I whisper back, "I don't know."

Elie goes to get a bar of dark chocolate from the cupboard and breaks off a big piece, which she hands to me. "Chocolate always cheers you up," she says.

I hate dark chocolate. I take a tiny bite and ask her, "Do you always ask so many nosy questions?"

"I'm afraid so. You can ask me a nosy question if you want, just for revenge.

"Uh . . . I don't want revenge."

With a mischievous grin, Elie shakes her right hand in my face.

"Surely you want to ask me about my hand. Everyone is curious about my hand," she says.

Once again, I don't know what to say. This girl is so blunt.

"How did it happen?" I ask.

She hesitates for a moment, then answers: "I was taking a walk and a wolf attacked me."

"Really?"

"No, I'm just kidding. I was born with only one hand. Simple as that."

The budgie leaves the top of the fridge and lands on Elie's shoulder.

"Hey, with your budgie like that, you look like our mayor. Have you seen her walking around with her parrot on her shoulder?"

"It's hard not to see her. She came to the cheese shop to show us her Senegal parrot. She talks to it like it's her baby."

Baby! Suddenly, I get another brilliant idea. I know how to get Tartatcheff to rent the arena to me. Let's do this, Madam Mayor!

Thomas: Where does the mayor leave the parrot during tai chi?

Sam: Home.

Thomas: Do your parents have a key to her house?

Sam: Yes.

Thomas: Great!

Sam: ???

Thomas: Will explain later. Meet you at the store.

Sam: Now!!!

Thomas : Patience.

Sam:

Ashes Are Better than Nothing at All

There is no trace of my mother at home. No photos. No dresses. (Did she wear dresses?) Not even an old pair of shoes stuffed at the bottom of a cupboard. My father got rid of everything.

Being wiped out is worse than dying. If my mother had died, we would surely have kept some pictures, a few pieces of jewelry. Even an urn filled with her ashes would have been better than this emptiness that hurts. With an urn, I could at least stop wondering where she is.

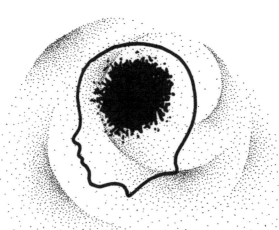

A Risky Business

By the time I get to the corner store, Sam is already there, licking his ice cream cone. I haven't even finished my explanation when he interrupts:

"You want to kidnap the mayor's parrot? Are you out of your mind? It's the thing she loves more than anything in the world!"

"Exactly," I reply. "We kidnap Tartatcheff's parrot and hide it for three days. Then we bring that disgusting bird back saying it was lost in the forest and we found it. The mayor will be so grateful to get her bird back that, as a token of thanks, she'll rent the arena to me for the PPP."

"And when do you want to do this?" asks Sam.

"Sunday morning," I reply. "Tartatcheff teaches her tai chi class on the lawn in front of City Hall. You said that she leaves her parrot in the enclosed porch and that your parents have the key."

"Too risky," says Sam.

"Are you scared?"

"If we get caught, we're dead. My parents are a lot stricter than your father . . ."

"I don't have a choice. No arena, no PPP."

Sam lets out a sigh. "If I agree to help you, you have to promise me that I'll get my picture in the *Guinness World Records* book."

"Okay, I promise. Cross my heart and hope to die."

From: ElieLadouce@mymail.ca
To: TomG@me.com
July 23, 10:41 a.m.

Hi, Mr. Poutine,

I finished reading *Asterix in Belgium*.

I understand why you like this comic since it explains how the Belgians invented French fries!

Here is the list of documents that you have to present in order to get your record officially recognized:

- Accompanying letter that describes the event and the record that was set.

- Two affidavits from witnesses who attended the event or one affidavit signed by a notary public. The witnesses must be over the age of eighteen and be certified in any one of the following professions: notary public, lawyer, police officer, or teacher.

- Media coverage as confirmation by a third party (newspaper article, video excerpt from a TV report, or audio from a radio report).

- Color photographs and video taken at the event.

Elie-your-devoted-PPP-organizer

P.S. You have lots of things to do and a lot of people to recruit to make your phenomenal poutine.

From: TomG@me.com
To: ElieLadouce@mymail.ca
July 23, 1:48 p.m.

Dear devoted organizer,

Thank you for your good work.

In return, you have the right to ask me one of your nosy questions.

Thomas-future-star-of-the-Guinness-World-Records.

She's right. I'm going to need an army of volunteers to get all this done.

If only my father could help me. If only he wasn't so obsessed with his sailboat. If only my father wasn't so uptight. If only my father acted like one.

Operation Kidnapping

Usually I sleep in till noon. But today I wake up at the same time as my father. The sun isn't even up yet. I'm too excited to sleep. When I come down to the kitchen, my father is finishing off his coffee and getting ready to leave for the bakery. He throws me a surprised look.

"Up already?"

"Yeah."

"To what do we owe this honor?"

"Nothing special."

My father doesn't insist. That's the problem in this house. Even the smallest question is swept under the rug. At our place, silence reigns supreme.

At eight o'clock sharp, I arrive at Sam's. He still has the creases of his pillowcase imprinted on his cheek.

"Don't make any noise. My parents are sleeping," he whispers.

We spy on the house next door from the basement window. At eight-thirty, the mayor takes her car to go and teach her tai chi class. As soon as she's turned the corner, we run to her place.

Just as Sam predicted, the mayor has left her parrot on the porch. And the door isn't even locked! George is calmly pecking away at a banana in his cage. Sam watches out as I throw a beach towel over the cage.

The back of Tartatcheff's house sits directly on a little forest. We go back to my place through this wooded area instead of by the road. During the whole trip, which takes about twenty minutes, George remains silent. Operation Kidnapping is a success! Whew!

I put the parrot's cage into the old shed at the bottom of our garden. The perfect hiding place because, since my father built his new workshop, he never goes there. The ugly bird can cackle all it wants; the shed is far enough away so that no one can hear him.

As soon as Sam takes the towel off the cage, George begins to holler:

"Rrrrradish . . . Rrrradish!"

Sam crouches down in front of the cage and slowly says:

"Madame Mayor has a big derrière."

"Rrrrradish . . . Rrrradish," repeats George.

"Why are you teaching him dumb insults?"

"So you think what the mayor has taught her parrot is smart? 'Cretin'? 'Celery brain'! That's polite?"

Hmmm. He's right. Thérèse Tartatcheff's sense of humor is a little twisted. Maybe she deserves a lesson. I go up to George and repeat louder and slower:

"Madame Mayor. Big derrière!"

"Rrrrradish . . . Rrrradish," repeats George stubbornly.

Sam shakes his head in disappointment:

"What an idiot!"

"Thomas? Thomas?"

That voice makes us jump like two terrified rabbits.

"Oops. It's Eliane Ladouceur."

"Hurry! Hide the parrot!" shouts Sam.

"No, we can let her in on it."

My friend looks at me as if I've suddenly sprouted a pink beard on my chin.

Into the Parrot's Mouth

From her raised eyebrows and crossed arms, I can see that Elie thinks I did a stupid thing kidnapping that disgusting bird.

"If anything happens to this parrot, you're as good as dead," she declares.

"We're only going to keep it for three days and then we'll take it back to the mayor. Promise. Cross my heart and hope to die."

Sam looks shyly at Elie. For once, he seems intimidated. Elie goes up to the cage.

"Hi, pretty George."

With its head to one side, the parrot stares at her intensely.

"Hi, pretty George," repeats Elie.

"Pretty George," says the parrot.

Elie's chocolate-colored braid hangs down to the bottom of her back. I wonder if she ever wears her hair loose, flying in the wind like in a shampoo commercial. She speaks softly to the bird.

"You're pretty, George. Come here."

"Pretty George," repeats the parrot.

Moving slowly, she opens the cage. The bird comes out and sits on her shoulder. Elie pats it gently.

"Wow! You really know about parrots!" exclaims Sam.

"Do you have any sunflower seeds?" Elie asks me.

"I don't eat bird food..."

"I'll bring some tomorrow. In the meantime, give him fruit," she says.

I make a face at the bird, who is still perched on Elie's shoulder.

"Does Mr. George want a rotten banana?"

"Total cretin!" answers the rude beast.

"Cretin yourself," I say, shaking my finger in his face.

With a sudden movement, the parrot stretches out its neck and bites my finger! Yow! Blood spurts everywhere. Elie puts the bird back in its cage. Then she wraps my finger with the bottom of my T-shirt and presses really tight.

"You must have frightened him. That's why he bit you," she explains.

"I'm going to have that turd of a bird stuffed."

"Do you have any peroxide in your bathroom?" asks Elie.

"I'll go and see," says Sam.

When he comes back with the peroxide and some bandages, Elie disinfects the bite.

"You're pretty good with both your hands!" declares Sam.

He blushes as soon as he says it.

I shake my head.

"You're really a moron."

Elie lifts her artificial hand in the air and laughs as she shakes her fingers.

"The advantage of an artificial hand is that the parrot can bite me and it won't hurt."

Quick—I need to find another subject.

"Do you think this parrot could have rabies?"

"No idea," answers Elie.

"What difference would it make? You're already crazy." Sam laughs.

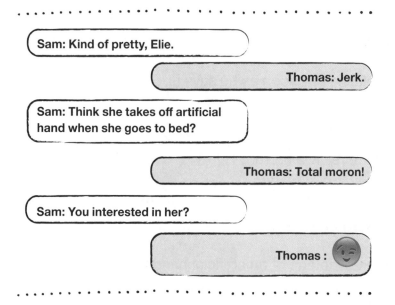

Sam: Kind of pretty, Elie.

Thomas: Jerk.

Sam: Think she takes off artificial hand when she goes to bed?

Thomas: Total moron!

Sam: You interested in her?

Thomas :

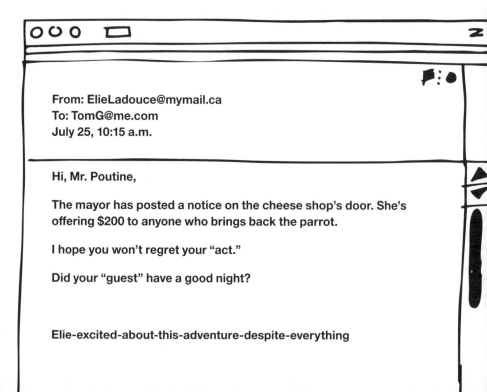

From: ElieLadouce@mymail.ca
To: TomG@me.com
July 25, 10:15 a.m.

Hi, Mr. Poutine,

The mayor has posted a notice on the cheese shop's door. She's offering $200 to anyone who brings back the parrot.

I hope you won't regret your "act."

Did your "guest" have a good night?

Elie-excited-about-this-adventure-despite-everything

From: TomG@me.com
To: ElieLadouce@mymail.ca
July 25, 11:10 a.m.

Dear organizer,

My "guest" shouts a little too much and a little too loud.
I can't wait to take him back.
When will you bring me the "food" you promised?

Thomas

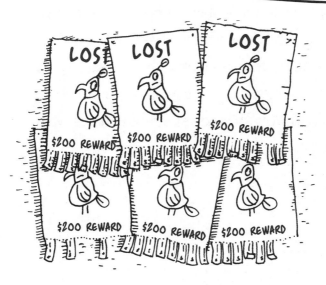

Real or Made-Up?

My mother didn't like the poutine at the arena. She called it a lazy man's poutine. If I had the choice, I'd also want homemade poutine. Not frozen fries, but golden ones, crispy on the outside and tender in the middle. Fresh cheese, not melted. And to finish off this perfect poutine, gravy that is neither too salty nor too sweet.

I think my mother made me homemade poutine, but I've forgotten so many things about her that maybe I'm making up stories without even realizing it. Like the business about the handcuffs. Did something really happen with handcuffs or is it just my supercharged imagination? Your mind does strange things when it's trying to fill a void . . .

Sam's Mistake

Elie, Sam, and I spend part of the afternoon in the shed feeding sunflower seeds to the parrot and trying to make it swear. But George is as stubborn as his owner and doesn't want to repeat what we're trying to teach him. He's happy croaking "Crrretin," or sometimes "Pretty George."

Elie and I go back into the house to get a snack. Even before I open the cupboard, Sam comes crashing into the kitchen in a panic.

"Come quick!"

"What?"

"The parrot! He's escaped!"

"WHAT?"

Elie and I rush to the shed. When I see the empty cage, I kick the door.

"Why did you let him out?"

Sheepishly, Sam answers:

"I wanted to copy Elie by putting him on my shoulder to help make him talk."

"If we don't find this bird, I'm going to murder you."

"He can't have gone too far. He's not used to being free."

"Exactly! Anything could happen to him."

We go around the property a few times, whispering, "George! George!"

We don't want to shout in case we attract the attention of my father who's in his workshop.

"Let's go and look by the woods," says Elie.

How Much Does a Parrot Cost?

As soon as we're ready to set off for the woods, Sam announces:

"I have to go. My mother's waiting for me. I have a dentist's appointment."

"Sure, go ahead and leave us to fix your mess."

"I can come back later."

No one answers him. He leaves.

"Come on," Elie says to me. "Bring the cage."

This girl thinks of everything.

At first we concentrate our search around the edge of the woods. Not the slightest sign. Not even the smallest parrot feather.

"We need to go farther into the forest," says Elie.

She leads the way while I follow carrying the cage. She calls out softly, "George! George!"

She whistles.

I'm hot, I'm thirsty, I'm beginning to get hungry, and I'm fed up with looking for this stupid bird.

"Should we take a break?" suggests Elie.

She sits down on a rock and takes out two bottles of water and two granola bars from her backpack. This girl really thinks of everything.

"What if he's taken off for Africa?"

Elie shoots me a questioning look.

"Yeah, well, it's a Senegal parrot."

"Very funny," says Elie without laughing.

"How long can a pet parrot survive in the wild?"

"No idea," replies Elie.

"Are parrots expensive?"

She looks at me as if I've just broken the record for the dumbest question of the century.

"It's obvious that you've never had a pet. You can't replace a parrot like you would a toaster."

I give the perch in the parrot's cage a flick of my finger. At this very moment, I would be thrilled to hear him call me a complete idiot.

Elie throws an acorn at me.

"Hey, can I ask you a personal question?"

I shrug my shoulders.

"If it makes you happy."

"Why is this Guinness world record so important to you?"

To stall for time, I take a long sip of water. How do you explain things that can't be explained?

"If I manage to make the biggest poutine in the world, and become somewhat famous, maybe my father will take more interest in me and maybe my mother will want to see me again . . ."

"You think you'll win your father's approval and that your mother will show up just because you're in the *Guinness World Records* book?"

"When I was little, my mother used to make homemade poutine. It's stupid, but I feel that by doing the PPP, I'm closer to her."

Elie twists the end of her braid.

"No, it's not stupid. With your PPP, it's like you're throwing a bottle into the sea with a message for your mother."

The idea of a bottle in the sea seems desperate and unrealistic. I'm neither one. I throw an acorn at Elie, who smiles and says, "You can ask me a personal question if you want."

"Where's your father?"

"He died when I was a baby . . ."

She looks at me defiantly.

"I was sure you were going to ask me about my hand."

Since she's given me an opening, I take advantage of it.

"Okay. I have a question about your hand. Do you take it off at night?

She bursts out laughing and answers:

"Of course. Every night I put my artificial hand in the dishwasher."

Panic in the Woods

We go in circles in the woods for almost an hour. Still no parrot to be seen.

I'm fed up with carrying the cage.

"Do you think he may have gone back to Tartatcheff's?"

"It's a parrot, not a homing pigeon," replies Elie.

Her curt tone shows how tired she is.

"Let's go and see," she says.

It takes us about ten minutes to get to Thérèse Tartatcheff's. Hidden behind a clump of trees, we can see the mayor sitting on her porch. No sign of the parrot.

"She looks so sad," whispers Elie. "We absolutely must return her George to her."

She goes back toward the woods, roughly moving aside the branches blocking her way. I let her go several meters ahead of me. Suddenly I see her jumping up and down and shouting.

As I run toward her, I notice some wasps. She must have disturbed a nest. So I don't excite the wasps any further, I slowly pull Elie away and make her sit down. She's moaning in pain. There are already two red splotches on her arm.

"I don't have my EpiPen."

"Your what?"

"EpiPen. My medication. I'm allergic to wasps."

Geez. We have to get out of here right now. I help her up, but she's unsteady. I can see in her eyes that she's scared.

"Thomas, my tongue is swelling up. I'm having trouble breathing."

Her lips look swollen. I'm beginning to panic.

"Call my mother . . ."

I take out my cell phone.

"Oh no!"

"What?" asks Elie in a feeble voice.

"The battery's dead."

She drops down right in the middle of the path. Tears are rolling down her cheeks.

"Can't . . . walk. Go to the mayor's. Closer. Call ambulance."

"You're not going to die, are you?"

What a ridiculous question. The parrot is right: I'm a complete idiot.

"Hurry!" whispers Elie.

The Biceps of a Weightlifter

The mayor is no longer on her porch. I ring the doorbell, twice, three times. I bang the door with my fists. When Tartatcheff finally arrives, I cry out:

"Quick! Call an ambulance!"

The mayor puts her hand on my shoulder:

"Calm down. Tell me what's wrong."

"Elie Ladouceur. Stung by wasps . . . Allergic reaction. Can't breathe . . ."

The mayor takes her phone out of her pocket, dials 911, and barks out her orders:

"An ambulance to 52 Forest Avenue, three kilometers south of Sainte-Alphonsine."

Then she hangs up.

"Let's go."

For such a big, husky woman, she runs fast. We find Elie sitting in the middle of the path, right where I left her a few minutes ago. She seems even weaker. The mayor bends down, feels her forehead, her arms.

Elie's eyes are closed. Her head looks as if it's too heavy for her neck. The mayor picks Elie up and heads back home. I've always made fun of how she looks like a lumberjack, but now her weightlifter's biceps are coming in very useful.

The mayor is walking quickly. Elie's head is rolling around. I hear the siren of the ambulance. There is no reaction from Elie. By the time we get to the mayor's, the ambulance drivers have already taken out the stretcher. Tartatcheff puts Elie down. One of the drivers takes her pulse. The other one puts an oxygen mask on her. I let out a scream:

"EtiPen! EtiPen!"

The guys throw me a strange look.

I turn to the mayor: "Quick! Your cell phone."

She gives me her phone and I dial Irene Ladouceur's number. When she answers, I pass the phone to the ambulance driver. I can't hear what she says, but the driver cries out to his colleague: "Epinephrine!"

The other one immediately jumps into action. I take Elie's hand. It's her artificial one, but I don't care. I don't want to let her go. In a shaky voice, I say to the ambulance drivers: "I'm going with her."

"You can't. If she gets worse, we'll need the space to move around."

"Please, let me come with you."

"Sorry," says the driver.

Tartatcheff tugs my T-shirt.

"Come on, kiddo. We'll go to the hospital together."

Laughing and Crying All at Once

Tartatcheff's car smells like rotten bananas. A pile of "Wanted" posters and a blow-up photo of the parrot take up the passenger seat. The mayor puts the photocopies on the backseat and, looking grief-stricken, she explains: "My George disappeared yesterday morning. I have to find him. I haven't been able to sleep. That bird is my family."

My heart starts beating frantically. I look down so that the mayor can't see my guilty look. "Sorry about your parrot."

That's the first sincere thing I've said to Tartatcheff, but she doesn't know that.

At the Granby hospital, a nurse lets us know that the doctor is already taking care of Elie. She sends us to the waiting room. Five minutes later, Irene Ladouceur storms in and rushes toward one of the examining rooms. The mayor is pacing like a mother lion in a cage.

"I can't stay long. I have some files to prepare for tomorrow," she says.

"Can I borrow your phone?" I ask.

I go down the hall to call home. Of course, my father doesn't answer. He must be in his workshop, fixing up his lousy sailboat. I give Tartatcheff her phone back.

"Thanks. My father is going to come and get me."

Luckily, the mayor doesn't notice that I'm lying. In any case, I'm not going to leave the hospital until I know how Elie is.

The mayor hands me her card: "Call to let me know how she's doing."

"Yes, ma'am. Thank you. Thank you for everything."

She already has her back to me, in a hurry to leave.

"Mrs. Tartatcheff!"

I catch up with her at the end of the hall.

"Uh . . . I'm really sorry about your parrot."

She passes her hand through her mop of red hair and says fiercely:

"I'm going to find my George! I just have to!"

I go back to the waiting room and wait impatiently. I bite my nails. An hour later, Irene Ladouceur finally comes out into the hall.

I run toward her. When she sees me, she starts crying and laughing at the same time. She gives me a big hug. She smells like old cheddar.

"Elie is feeling better. This could have been very serious. The doctor wants to keep her overnight for observation. I'm going to stay with her."

PHEW
PHEW
PHEW
PHEW

I stop myself from dancing. From singing. I feel like kissing the nurse with the white hair. And the receptionist with her big square glasses. I feel like kissing the coffee machine!

A Candy-Pink Note

I've used the receptionist's phone three times to call my father. He still doesn't answer. I'm exhausted, I'm dying of hunger, and it would take me all night to get home on foot. I finally decide to call Sam. I'm relieved to hear Léa's voice. There's no need to go into long explanations with her.

"Don't move," she says. "I'm coming."

Less than a half hour later, Sam's mother arrives at the hospital. I crash with relief into the passenger seat. I don't have a single ounce of energy left.

Léa hands me a ham sandwich and a bottle of grape juice.

"Eat. Then you'll tell me everything."

I'm in the middle of the second half of my sandwich when my eye catches a candy-pink Post-it note stuck on the dashboard. I recognize Léa's handwriting:

My heart starts beating like crazy. That color reminds me . . . reminds me . . . candy pink! At that moment, I get it. I open the window and throw out the rest of the sandwich.

"Hey!" protests Léa.

I turn to her:

"The envelopes, for my birthday. It's you, isn't it? You're the one who's been putting them in my mailbox."

I shouldn't yell, but I can't contain the rage that's come over me. Léa drives toward the shoulder and stops the car. I scream again:

"Why have you been pretending to be my mother?"

"Calm down, Thomas."

"Who do you think you are—my fairy godmother? A little gift for poor Thomas? Your pity makes me sick!"

Léa puts her hand on my shoulder, but I push her away roughly.

"Thomas, it really is your mother who's been sending you the money. And the messages too. Except for the last one on the pink paper. I'm the one who added it."

"Why doesn't she send them herself, those stupid letters?"

"She doesn't want you to be able to track her down."

"Why?"

"Thomas, I can't explain it to you."

"I want to know."

"I know. You have the right to know. But your father's the one who has to tell you."

"He doesn't want to! He couldn't care less!"

Léa puts her forehead on the steering wheel.

"He does care. He's hurt. Ask him to explain it to you. If he refuses, I will. Okay?"

She restarts the car. The rest of the way passes in silence. When I get home, I turn to Léa:

"Just tell me one thing. The handcuffs. Was my mother handcuffed?"

Léa doesn't say anything. She doesn't need to. Her pained look is my answer.

Handcuffed for Agression

I rush into the workshop where I find my father fast asleep in his sailboat.

Seeing him sleep so peacefully just makes me angrier. While I'm at the hospital after saving Elie's life, Mr. Big Shot here is snoring. I called him five thousand times from the hospital, but he was snoozing instead of answering. He must hold the record for the most useless father in the world. Never there when I need him.

I pick up a piece of wood and let it fall on the floor. My father wakes with a start. I ask my question right in his face:

"Why did they handcuff my mother?"

My father turns pale. His shoulders drop. He looks as if he's just seen a ghost.

"Who told you?"

"Léa Bernier."

"Why is she butting in?"

"In fact, Léa doesn't want to butt in. She says it's up to you to explain everything to me."

My father gets out of his sailboat. I follow him into the house.

"Tell me."

He shakes his head.

"You don't want to know."

"You've hidden the truth from me for years. I'm twelve years old. I'm not a baby anymore. I WANT TO KNOW."

My father pours himself a glass of water. He drinks slowly to stall for time. I grip the back of a chair to stop myself from shaking. My father sits down at the table. Without looking at me, he says in a flat voice:

"Your mother drank too much. For a long time. She also took medication for depression. When you were four years old, she drove, drunk, to the mall. It was summer and very hot . . . She forgot you in the car with the doors locked."

He rubs his eyes with his fists as if he's trying to erase this memory.

"And then?"

"A passerby called the police. They smashed the window to get you out of the car. No one knows how long you had been there, but you were already dehydrated."

"And the handcuffs?"

"Your mother got back to the car just as the police were

taking you away. She had a fit, insisted on taking you home. She was being aggressive, so the police were forced to handcuff her."

There's not a sound in the kitchen. I'm no longer shaking. I sit down, stunned.

"And then?"

"Your mother was charged with drunk driving and criminal negligence. It wasn't the first time she was found guilty of drunk driving. Because of her previous convictions, the judge was harsh. Your mother was sent to jail for eight months."

"Go on."

"When she got out of prison, she came back to Sainte-Alphonsine, just for a few weeks. She didn't want to stay."

"Why not?"

"Shame. She was ashamed to show her face in the village, ashamed of being a bad mother, ashamed because of the booze. She began to drink again. She left on the night of your fifth birthday."

"Where does she live?"

"In Montreal."

"What does she do there?"

"Nothing. She drinks."

"Why doesn't she want to see me?"

"Thomas, do I have to draw you a picture? Your mother is an alcoholic. She destroys everything she touches."

I've kept the hardest question for last. I might cause a volcano. Tough. I.WANT.TO.KNOW.

"Why do you hate her so much?"

My father turns red, scrunches up his eyes, his cheeks, his whole face. But he holds back his tears and spits out his answer in an angry voice:

"Because she abandoned us."

A Screech in the Night

With his elbows on the table, my father holds his head in his hands. Before, he didn't know how to tell me the truth. Now that I know the truth, he doesn't know how to console me.

Suddenly, the anger that was churning up my insides disappears. I go up to my room, drop onto my bed, and take my shoes off. Certain images are whirling around in my head.

A little kid locked in a car. With the sun beating down. The heat. Intense. Is the kid frightened? Is he crying? I don't know. I don't remember a thing.

I'd like to turn my brain off, stop the thought machine. Impossible. After I've been tossing and turning in bed, my sheets are sweaty.

I get up and take the old shoe box out of the cupboard.

In the hall, I notice a ray of light under my father's door. Is that sobbing I hear? The volcano took time to react. I couldn't care less.

The very round, very white moon lights up the lawn behind the house perfectly. The grass feels cool on my bare feet. I lift the garbage can lid and throw in the cardboard box with the five pine-green candles. I don't cry. There's no volcano in me. No rage. No sadness. NOTHING. I've turned into a zombie. I'm not here. Even the emptiness that hurts has disappeared.

Suddenly, a screech makes me jump:

"Crrrretin! Total crrrretin!"

A few steps away, perched in the apple tree, Thérèse Tartatcheff's parrot is shaking his feathers.

I Don't Feel Anything

When I wake up the next morning, I feel the same sense of emptiness as when I went to bed the night before. I have no energy. My body feels heavy and limp. I don't feel anything. Everything turns me off.

I drag myself to the phone and call Irene Ladouceur.

"It's Thomas Gagné."

"Hi, Thomas Gagné."

"Uh . . . Elie ?"

"Everything's fine. She's getting out of the hospital this morning."

"Can you please give her a message from me? Tell her that I've found what I was looking for. Everything is back where it belongs."

"I'll give her the message. Are you going to come over to see her this afternoon?" asks Irene Ladouceur.

I say yes, but I'm not going to. I don't want to see anyone. I want to turn into a turtle and disappear under my shell.

Sam: Mom told me about Elie. Any news?

Thomas: Out of hospital this morning.

Sam: 😜

Sam: George came back! Neighbor crazy happy.

Thomas: I know. I brought him back.

Sam: Is T. renting the arena to you?

Thomas: PPP cancelled.

Sam: Cancelled?????????

Thomas: DON'T WANT TO TALK ABOUT IT.

Sam: 😟

A Mummy in Bed

Sam's text message reminds me about my promise to the mayor. I take her card out of my pocket and phone her.

"Hello! Hello!" she answers in a cheery voice.

"It's Thomas Gagné."

"Oh yes, handsome Thomas who runs in the woods!"

The mayor is calling me "handsome Thomas"?

"Elie Ladouceur is getting out of the hospital this morning."

"Wonderful! Everything's great! Thomas, I've found my parrot. George has come back. Life is grand!"

Thérèse Tartatcheff is speaking so loudly that it's giving me a headache. Her happiness makes me sick.

"I'm happy for you."

As soon as I hang up, the phone rings. Then my cell

phone starts to ring. I don't answer. They keep on ringing. That Sam sure is persistent. I unplug the phone and turn off my cell. Wrapped up in my sheet like a mummy, I play dead. I wish I were a real mummy in a sarcophagus—a complete void inside and totally dark on the outside.

Later, the doorbell rings. And rings and rings. Stubborn Sam. I still play dead. I must have fallen asleep because my father wakes me up when he gets home from the bakery. He looks worried.

"What are you doing in bed at 2:00 in the afternoon?"

". . ."

"Are you sick?"

"No."

"Sam is here."

"I don't want to see anyone."

My father remains planted in the middle of my room, as affectionate as a block of concrete. Finally, almost against his will, he asks:

"Is it because of last night?"

"Tell Sam I'm sick."

My father leaves without saying another word. Two minutes later, Sam comes running up the stairs. Not only is my father indifferent and useless, he's a traitor.

Still a Zombie

Standing at the foot of my bed, Sam stares at me with a worried look.

"What's going on?"

I pull the sheet over my head.

"Tired."

"Why aren't you answering the phone or the door?"

"T-i-r-e-d. I was up late last night because of some idiot who let the mayor's obnoxious bird escape." Sam shifts from one foot to the other.

"How did you find the freaking bird?"

"He came back by himself last night. Since the cage was still in the forest and I wasn't going to go back there in the middle of the night, I got a big cardboard box from the shed. I managed to get the bird in it without him tearing off a finger. I left George on Tartatcheff's porch, making sure to close the door behind me."

Sam looks stunned.

"You were supposed to tell her that you saved her parrot so that she would rent out the arena to you for the PPP. And you didn't even tell her that you found her George? I don't get it."

"It's over. I'm not doing the PPP."

I can see that my friend is making an enormous effort not to get angry. His frustration means nothing to me. I'm indifferent. He doesn't say a word about my mother. I figure that his mother didn't tell him about our conversation.

"And what about our picture in the *Guinness World Records* book?"

"I don't care about your dumb picture!"

"And what about the soccer team? And your sponsors? What are you going to tell all of them?"

"Who cares. It's all over. FINISHED!"

Sam raises both hands.

"I don't know what your problem is. I'll come back when you're ready to talk. But I'm warning you, Thomas Gagné, the PPP is not over."

He slams the door on his way out. I don't even flinch. I'm still like a zombie. Still as empty.

From: ElieLadouce@mymail.ca
To: TomG@me.com
July 26, 4:37 p.m.

Dear Mr. Poutine,

My mother told me that you found the you-know-what.

I'm very, very, very happy.

BUT, I am not at all happy to hear that you've called off the PPP!

Tell me it's not true.

I spent hours organizing all the Guinness forms.

I got bitten by wasps because of your stupid plan to kidnap you-know-what.

After all that,
you CANNOT cancel.

Frustrated-Elie

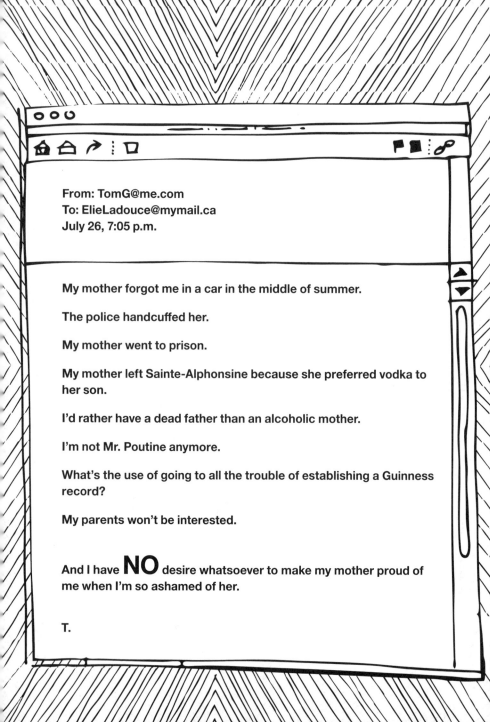

From: TomG@me.com
To: ElieLadouce@mymail.ca
July 26, 7:05 p.m.

My mother forgot me in a car in the middle of summer.

The police handcuffed her.

My mother went to prison.

My mother left Sainte-Alphonsine because she preferred vodka to her son.

I'd rather have a dead father than an alcoholic mother.

I'm not Mr. Poutine anymore.

What's the use of going to all the trouble of establishing a Guinness record?

My parents won't be interested.

And I have **NO** desire whatsoever to make my mother proud of me when I'm so ashamed of her.

T.

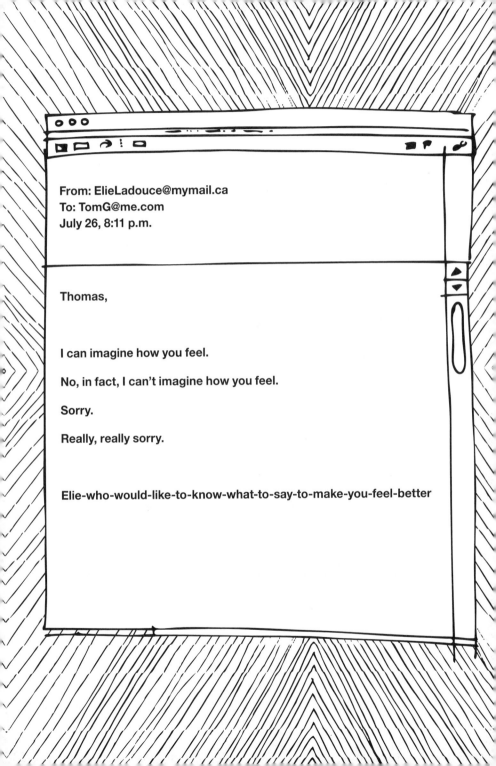

From: ElieLadouce@mymail.ca
To: TomG@me.com
July 26, 8:11 p.m.

Thomas,

I can imagine how you feel.

No, in fact, I can't imagine how you feel.

Sorry.

Really, really sorry.

Elie-who-would-like-to-know-what-to-say-to-make-you-feel-better

Clean Dishes

Two days after admitting that she's been in contact with my mother, Léa Bernier comes to the door. Sam must have told her that I don't answer his calls or his text messages. It's not even eight o'clock. I haven't had breakfast and I don't feel like talking to anyone. And my father isn't even here to make excuses for me. I run and hide in my room. I hear Sam's mother come into the house.

"Thomas? Thomas?"

I don't answer. I wait. I hear her running the water in the kitchen sink. She's doing the dishes! She's as stubborn as her neighbor Tartatcheff. I decide to go downstairs. When she sees me, Sam's mother reaches out with her suds-covered hands. I draw back. My zombie doesn't want to be touched. She asks gently:

"Your father told you everything?"

"Yes."

"Do you want to talk about it?"

"No."

She's twisting the tea towel. I can feel her discomfort, but I don't care.

"Thomas, alcoholism is a disease. Your mother is very sick."

"I don't give a crap."

Léa goes on as if she didn't hear me:

"I haven't spoken to your mother much for the last few years. She refuses my help. The only thing she asks is that I give you the money and her message for your birthday."

"Stop. I don't want to know."

"Okay. I'll stop. But just one more thing before I do. When your mother left Sainte-Alphonsine, she said something that I want to repeat now. She said, 'I love my son. I love him so much that I want to get out of his life.'"

She waits for an answer. I react with a stony silence. Is she going to realize that I want her to leave?

"Fine. I'll leave you now . . ."

". . ."

She takes one step toward me.

"Would you like a big hug?"

I draw back.

"No!"

Léa looks sad. She should just mind her own business, whispers my zombie. She leaves, closing the door softly. The dishes she washed are drying on the counter. I don't even feel like breaking a plate. I don't feel anything.

Sam: Can we talk about PPP?

Thomas: PPP is cancelled. End of story.

Sam: ????????

Thomas: You could have told me that my mother was an alcoholic.

Sam: What are you talking about????

Sam: Can I come over?

Sam: Thomas!!! Answer me!

Sam: Why aren't you answering?

Creak, Creak or Squeak, Squeak?

I turn off my cell, unplug the phone, and go back to bed. My father's working at the bakery. No one to tell me to eat. To breathe. No one to tell me what to do to get rid of this empty feeling inside.

Around three o'clock, voices wake me up. They're coming from the kitchen. I recognize my father's voice but not the woman's. I go down the first three steps of the staircase. I can see the tops of their heads: my father's salt-and-pepper hair and her hair, the color of chocolate. My father puts his foot on the first step and calls up:

"Thomas, there's someone here to see you."

When I join them in the kitchen, my father gives me a strange look. I can't tell if he's angry, surprised, or disappointed. I wonder if Irene Ladouceur has told him everything.

"I'll let you two talk," he mumbles, before escaping to his workshop.

Irene Ladouceur smiles at me:

"Hi, Thomas."

I can tell by her smile of worry mixed with pity that Elie has told her everything. She hands me a bag of cheese curds.

"A snack for you."

"Thanks."

"May I sit down? I won't be long."

I show her to the living room. She sits down on the sofa and I take a chair, as far away as possible.

Don't let her near you, whispers my zombie.

"You told my father everything?"

"Not everything. The poutine, yes; the kidnapping, no. I haven't come to talk about the past, but about the future."

". . ."

"Elie tells me that the mayor refuses to rent the arena to you for your Guinness record. I have an idea to fix your problem. In a few weeks, it'll be the Granby International, the antique car show. You could rent a six-by-twelve-meter tent, big enough for standing room for twenty-five people. You could set up your hot plates and serve your giant poutine."

"I don't have enough money to rent a tent . . ."

"I've spoken to Frank, the owner of Fat Frank's Fries. He's agreed to pay for half the cost of renting the tent. I'll give you 25 percent. Since the media will be there, we'll put it in our advertising budget. You can make up the difference with the money you've collected."

". . ."

"This show is the ideal place for your PPP. All the journalists go to it, so it'll be easy to get them to come and see the giant poutine. And they're expecting 25,000 visitors. Tons of people to eat your 650-kilo poutine."

I don't react. My zombie is still in charge.

"So? What do you say?"

"I told Elie and I'm telling you: I'm not doing the PPP. I don't care about the Guinness record."

Irene Ladouceur opens the bag of cheese curds, takes one, and chews it slowly.

"Can you hear the *creak*, *creak*? That means it's really fresh."

All of a sudden, I'm five years old. The pine-green candles are lighting up the poutine. I hear my mother's voice: "If the curds go *squeak*, *squeak* when you eat them, that means they're fresh."

Irene Ladouceur's innocent comment hits me full force.
I stammer:

"My—my—my mother said—my mother used to say
'squeak, squeak,' not 'creak, creak.'"

As I say *squeak, squeak*, I let out a little ironic laugh.
This laugh sets off a shaking inside, in my guts. Then
on the outside. I grip the arm of my chair.

"I'm so . . . ashamed of my mother . . . but I really . . .
want . . . to see her again."

Irene Ladouceur crouches down in front of me and
stares at me intensely. Her eyes aren't the same blue as
Elie's.

"Even when a mother makes mistakes, even when she's
hurt, neglectful, damaged, or sick, her child has the
right to love her."

A sound comes out of my throat, something between a
groan and a sigh. My shoulders are shuddering. A stream
of salty tears covers my face. A tsunami of tears.

Irene Ladouceur puts her arms around me. She doesn't give me a bear hug, but rocks me gently. She still smells like old cheddar. I hope she doesn't tell Elie that I drenched her blouse with tears.

Goodbye, zombie.

Crying hurts.

Not just a little.

A lot.

But it's better than not feeling anything at all.

Challenges Are Good for You

After Irene Ladouceur leaves, I play Angry Birds. A good way not to have to think about her offer. An hour later, my father comes up to my room and puts a still warm grilled cheese sandwich in front of me. He sits down on my bed:

"Why didn't you say anything about your plans for the Guinness world record?"

I shrug my shoulders.

"Everyone has their secrets."

He takes the jab without a word. Then he takes several $50 bills out of his pocket and puts them on my dresser.

"Here's my contribution for renting the tent."

"Too late. I've dropped the PPP."

My father shakes his head.

"Is it because of your mother?"

". . ."

My father bends down toward me. Is he going to touch me? No.

"Don't give up your plans, Thomas."

"Why not?"

"It's good to challenge yourself. To have dreams to fulfill."

". . ."

"If you ever change your mind, I'd like to help you make the biggest poutine in the world," says my father.

I'm so shocked I almost fall off my chair.

Stale Fries

I go back to my game of Angry Birds. Click, click, click
. . . I try not to think, but it's getting harder and harder
since my zombie left. An hour later, thirst finally forces
me to leave my computer. My father has once again
disappeared into his workshop. A brown paper bag sits
on top of the kitchen table, with a candy-pink piece of
paper stuck on it.

FOR THE GUINNESS,
I FEEL LIKE GIVING YOU A KICK IN
THE PANTS AND SAYING
YOU CAN DO IT!
AS FOR YOUR MOTHER, IF IT HELPS,
I'M READY TO LISTEN.
SAM.

In the bag, poutine with dried-out gravy and stale fries.

. . . . · . . . .

Thomas: Your poutine was cold.
Thanks anyway.

Sam: 😄

Disappearing Garbage

I roll over and over in bed, just like a crepe. Can't sleep. I'm thinking of everyone who has shown up in the last two days. There sure are a lot of people who want to help: Sam, Léa, Elie, Irene, Fat Frank. Even my father. Can I disappoint all of them?

Plus, I'd like to prove to everyone—especially Thérèse Tartatcheff—that I'm capable of creating this 650-kilo poutine. And it would be exciting to see myself in the *Guinness World Records* book.

Finally, I go out. I put on a pair of work gloves and open the garbage can. I move the garbage around in vain. There's no sign of the pine-green candles. I turn the garbage can upside down. Still not even the tiniest bit of a candle. Strange.

Back in bed, I dream about a poutine as high as Mount Everest.

When I wake up, my mind is made up.

. . . .

Thomas: Still want your picture in the *Guinness World Records*?

Sam: YES!!!!

Thomas: I'm going to start up the PPP again.

Sam: Are you going to change your mind again?

Thomas: No.

Sam: I'm coming!!!

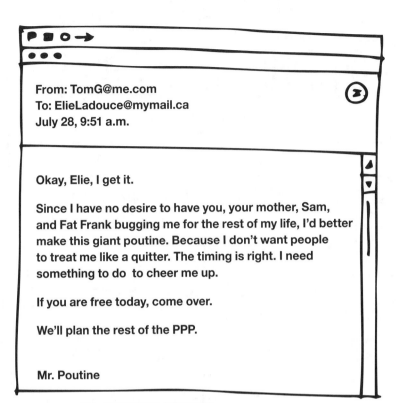

From: TomG@me.com
To: ElieLadouce@mymail.ca
July 28, 9:51 a.m.

Okay, Elie, I get it.

Since I have no desire to have you, your mother, Sam,
and Fat Frank bugging me for the rest of my life, I'd better
make this giant poutine. Because I don't want people
to treat me like a quitter. The timing is right. I need
something to do to cheer me up.

If you are free today, come over.

We'll plan the rest of the PPP.

Mr. Poutine

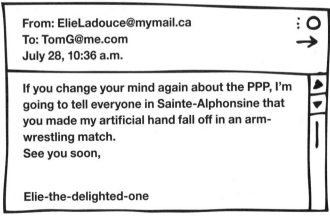

From: ElieLadouce@mymail.ca
To: TomG@me.com
July 28, 10:36 a.m.

If you change your mind again about the PPP, I'm
going to tell everyone in Sainte-Alphonsine that
you made my artificial hand fall off in an arm-
wrestling match.
See you soon,

Elie-the-delighted-one

OUTLINE

FOR THE PRODUCTION OF THE BIGGEST POUTINE IN THE WORLD

 FRIDAY, AUGUST 12

TASKS	IN CHARGE
GO TO GRANBY TO RENT HOT PLATES FOR THE GRAVY. SET UP THE TENT.	FAT FRANK, IRENE LADOUCEUR, THOMAS, SAM, ELIE, PIERRE GAGNÉ

SUNDAY, AUGUST 14

10:00 A.M. EQUIPMENT SET-UP: (metal table, hot plates for fries and gravy, butcher's scale, kitchen utensils, etc.) in Granby.	THOMAS, SAM, ELIE, PIERRE GAGNÉ, LÉA BERNIER, SOCCER TEAM
10:00 A.M. SPONSORS DELIVER CHEESE AND PRE-COOKED FRIES..	IRENE LADOUCEUR, FAT FRANK
10:40 A.M. WEIGH ALL THE INGREDIENTS: FRIES, CHEESE, AND GRAVY. FILM THE WEIGH-IN.	THOMAS, SAM, ELIE, WITH NOTARY PUBLIC AS WITNESS VIDEO: PIERRE GAGNÉ.

11:15 A.M. REHEAT THE GRAVY AND THE PRE-COOKED FRIES..	FAT FRANK, LÉA BERNIER
11:30 A.M. SET UP POUTINE ON BIG METAL TABLE SPREAD OUT FRIES AND CHEESE, AND POUR GRAVY OVER EVERYTHING.	THOMAS, SAM, ELIE, IRENE LADOUCEUR
TAKE OFFICIAL PHOTO FOR *GUINNESS WORLD RECORDS*.	PIERRE GAGNÉ NOTE: TRY TO TAKE THIS PICTURE WHEN SAM IS BUSY SOMEWHERE ELSE.
12:00 NOON START TO SERVE THE POUTINE..	GU PA
DURING THE DAY FILM ALL THE PREPARATIONS AND THE EVENT FROM START TO FINISH, INCLUDING THE CROWD STUFFING THEMSELVES WITH POUTINE. TAKE ALL THE PHOTOS NEEDED TO AUTHENTICATE THE RECORD..	PIER
5:00 P.M. CLEAN UP TENT AND GROUNDS AND COLLECT ALL THE CRAP THAT THE CROWD LEFT BEHIND.	SAM.

THOMAS GAGNÉ, YOU SCUMBAG, IF YOU TRY TO PLAY THIS TRICK ON ME, I'LL DUMP YOUR 650-KILO POUTINE ON YOUR HEAD. SAM.

THOMAS GAGNÉ, YOU USELESS TWIT, I'M NOT YOUR CLEANING LADY!!!

It took Elie, Sam, and me two hours to prepare this chart. I hope I didn't forget anything. That's a lot of people to manage and a lot of things to think about.

Few Words, Lots of Silence

"Dad?"

"What?"

"Are you going to forgive her someday?"

Thirty seconds of silence. My father shakes his head:

"I can't."

"Well, I'm starting to forgive her."

Twenty-five seconds of silence. My father says halfheartedly:

"I guess it's probably better that way . . ."

Thirty seconds of silence.

"Dad . . . I'd still like to see her again."

"I know."

Fifty seconds of silence.

"Can I?"

"If you want. And as long as she wants to . . ."

A boy from Sainte-Alphonsine could very well find himse
Guinness World Records book with quite an unusual reco
biggest poutine in the world. 650 kilos! Yesterday, with
of his soccer team and a small army of volunteers, 12-ye
Thomas Gagné served his poutine to more than 950 peo

THE BIGGES
IN THE

650 KG

T POUTINE
WORLD

two main sponsors of the
ent were Frank Beaumont,
er of Fat Frank's Fries, who
ated 300 kilos of French fries,
Ladouceur's Cheese Shop with
generous donation of 150 kilos
cheese curds. Thomas's father
vered the cost of the gravy. It all
ok place yesterday under a big
ent, as part of the Granby International, the annual antique car show.
A notary from Sainte-Alphonsine

was there to authenticate the
weight of the poutine. "The entire
project was completed according
to the rules set out by Guinness,"
confirmed the notary.
The duly signed documents will
be sent to the Guinness World
Records in England. In one month
from now, young Gagné will learn
if he has set the new record for the
biggest poutine in the world.

Elie's Questions

The lemonade is fresh and the sun is warm. It feels good to be sitting on the steps in front of Elie Ladouceur's house.

"So, Mr. Poutine, what was the best thing that happened during your big day?" asks Elie.

"I don't know. I'm just relieved that I managed to get a team together to make and serve a 650-kilo poutine without any hitches, or accidents, or big mistakes."

"The fries could have been hotter . . ."

"Yeah . . . But what bugged me the most were the idiots who kept butting in line for their free poutine. And Sam, who asked me at least ten thousand times when they were going to take the official photo for the *Guinness World Records* book."

"Yeah, I could see that you were pretty nervous, especially around the reporters. You kept stumbling when you answered their questions."

"Really?"

Elie taps me on the shoulder.

"Of course not. I'm just teasing, silly. Hey, your father stayed from the beginning right to the end. Are you happy?"

"You and your personal questions . . ."

Elie smiles.

"Yes, I was happy that my father was there and that he filmed everything. I was also happy to see the guys from the soccer team kidding around with you."

Elie blushes, then quickly changes the subject:

"The thing I'll never forget is when Thérèse Tartatcheff showed up with George on her shoulder. And when the parrot saw Sam, he began to cry out, as clear as a radio announcer: 'Mayor Big Derrière!'"

A New Project

This morning, I found an envelope addressed to me on the kitchen table. Inside were the five pine-green candles. On a piece of paper, my father wrote my mother's name with her address and telephone number in Montreal.

Now that I've established my Guinness world record, I'm ready to take on a new challenge.